Published by Scholastic Inc., 90 Old Sherman Turnpike, Danbury, Connecticut 06816.

For information regarding permission, write to:
Disney Licensed Publishing, 114 Fifth Avenue, New York, New York 10011

ISBN 0-7172-6752-0

Printed in the U.S.A.
First printing, June 2003

Disney's Piglet's BIG MOVIE

SCHOLASTIC INC.

New York Toronto London Auckland Sydney
Mexico City New Delhi Hong Kong Buenos Aires

It was a very busy day in the Hundred-Acre Wood.
Piglet was making a scrapbook inside his snug little
house. He gathered his drawings into a book to
remember all the fun times with his friends.

Piglet looked up to see Rabbit strolling past the
window carrying a violin. Next came Pooh, holding a
big pot. Eeyore, who was dressed like a bee, followed.
Then Piglet saw a tree walking by. Ah . . . no! That
wasn't a tree! It was Tigger wearing a tree costume.

Piglet hurried outside to find out what his friends
were doing.

When Piglet found his friends, Rabbit was in a tree, playing the violin to a beehive.

"Rabbit, what are you doing?" asked Piglet.

"I'm lull-a-by-ing the bees," answered Rabbit, "for our big plan."

"Eeyore, what are you doing?" Piglet asked.

"I'm using my BIG voice to tell the bees about their new hive," explained Eeyore.

"Tigger, could you tell me what you're doing?" asked Piglet.

"I have to hold the fake hive high enough for the bees to see," said Tigger. "It's the BIGGEST part of the plan!"

Finally, Piglet asked Pooh, "What are you all doing?"

"Harvesting honey, of course," answered Pooh. "It's all in the plan!"

"Can I help you with your big plan?"
asked Piglet.

"Well, thank you,
Piglet," said Pooh. "Um,
perhaps another time."

"When we have a bit smaller of a plan,"
added Tigger, "or when you're a bit bigger
of a piglet."

"I am very sorry, Piglet," said Rabbit.
"But I'm afraid this is a very big plan."

Poor Piglet! He
wanted to be a part
of the big plan, too!

Just then the friends heard a loud
buzzing coming from inside the hive. Rabbit's violin
playing must have annoyed the bees, because suddenly
the bees shot out of the hive. And they were very angry!

"*BUZZZZ!*" The bees flew right into Eeyore's megaphone, which was pointed at his mouth! Piglet quickly grabbed the megaphone and used it to lead the bees into the fake hive. Then Piglet sealed the bees inside with a gluey piece of paper.

But nobody noticed that
Piglet had saved his friends
from the angry bees.

"Our plan
worked perfectly!"
shouted Rabbit.

"Hoo-hoo-HOO!
Hooray for Pooh!"
cried Tigger.

"And Rabbit,"
added Pooh.

"And Eeyore," added Rabbit.

"And Tigger, too," said Eeyore.

"But, but . . . I was the . . . ," Piglet
started to say. But none of his friends heard.
They were too busy celebrating and
congratulating themselves.

A little later, Piglet walked through the Hundred-Acre Wood all by himself, feeling small and unimportant.

"It would sure be nice if my friends needed me," he murmured. When Piglet's scarf got caught on a fence, he didn't even notice. He just kept walking.

Meanwhile, at the honey celebration, the fake hive began buzzing louder and louder. It shook, then rumbled, and finally exploded. The very, very angry bees flew out.

Rabbit looked up and saw this. He said urgently, "What say we break for lunch?"

"But what about our honey?" asked Pooh.

"It's your honey or your life!" yelled Rabbit, as he took off running.

"Oh, bother!" said Pooh.

"Whoa!" cried Tigger.

"Quick! Make a beeline for Piglet's!" shouted Rabbit.

Pooh, Tigger, and Rabbit ran into Piglet's house and slammed the door just in time. The bees rumbled on the other side of the door. Suddenly it became quiet. Then the doorknob slowly turned.

The three friends ducked under the blankets and peeked out. The door opened. It was Eeyore—with a big bump on his nose!

"Eeyore!" said Pooh. "You got stung out there?"

"No, I got stung right here," answered Eeyore, "where I can keep an eye on it."

Tigger discovered Piglet's scrapbook. Everyone gathered around to look at it.

Then Rabbit said, "Where is Piglet?"

"Hoo! We must have lost track of him after we got chased by the bees," said Tigger.

"We have to find him and make sure he is all right," said Pooh.

"But how will we find him?" asked Rabbit.

"Since this is a book of Piglet's memories, maybe it remembers where Piglet is," said Pooh.

Pooh opened Piglet's scrapbook and saw a drawing of Kanga and Roo.

"Well then, Kanga's house is where we'll look for Piglet!" announced Rabbit.

"Piglet has always liked visiting Kanga's," said Pooh.

"Not always," remarked Eeyore.

"Oh, yes," remembered Pooh. "When Kanga and Roo first moved to the Hundred-Acre Wood . . . "

Tigger opened the scrapbook to a drawing of Kanga moving in. "There it is," he said.

So, as the friends headed to Kanga's house to find Piglet, they told the story of Kanga and Roo's first day in the Hundred-Acre Wood.

One sunny day in the Hundred-Acre Wood, Pooh and his friends hid in the tall grass and secretly watched the new family settling in.

"I've never seen anything like it!" declared Rabbit.

Just then Roo jumped into Kanga's pouch and disappeared. Pooh, Piglet, and Tigger gasped!

"She swallowed him whole!" Rabbit exclaimed.

Even though Roo later reappeared, the friends still didn't trust the newcomers.

"I tell you, we won't be safe until they're out, out of the Hundred-Acre Wood!" declared Rabbit. "Fortunately, I have a plan."

Rabbit explained his plan. Pooh would distract Kanga, while Rabbit ran off with Roo. Then Tigger would slip Piglet into Kanga's pouch.

When Kanga discovered the switch, the group would refuse to give Roo back until Kanga promised to leave the Hundred-Acre Wood and never return!

Pooh and his friends marched over to Kanga's to carry out their plan.

"Come on, Roo," called Kanga. "Hop in! Let's go inside."

"Oh, Kanga . . . um . . . ," said Pooh, "I was just wondering . . . uh . . . is that a fish in that tree?"

While Pooh distracted Kanga by asking her silly questions, Tigger tucked Piglet inside Kanga's pouch.

"Snug as a piggie in a blankie!" said Tigger.

Kanga was surprised
when she discovered Piglet
inside her pouch instead
of her little Roo. But she
pretended not to notice.
She just went about her
motherly tasks as usual.

AAAAAGHH!

"I'm going to give you a
bath," said Kanga.
Piglet did not
like baths!
But Kanga
scrubbed him clean
anyway. And then
she dried him until
he was fluffy!

AHHH-
CHOO!

"There are always two things you get after your bath, Roo," said Kanga. "A cookie. And a kiss." Then Kanga gave Piglet one of each!

At the end of the story, Pooh said, "You see, if it weren't for Piglet, we never would have found out how nice Kanga is."

"We'd never have had any of Kanga's songs," said Eeyore.

"Or her hugs," sniffed Tigger, with tears in his eyes.

"Or her cookies," said Pooh, "which my nose is telling my tummy are right nearby!"

"Kanga, we're so glad you didn't leave,"
blubbered Tigger.

"What are you talking about, Tigger?" asked
Kanga, a little confused.

"How Piglet took a bath for us," explained Rabbit.

"Not just any-ol'-body'd do something that brave
for his friends," said Tigger.

"Don't know if I would," remarked Eeyore.

"And we're ever so worried about him, you see,"
explained Pooh. "So we're using his book of
memories to find him."

Kanga said it was okay for Roo to help his friends look for Piglet. She gave each of them a cookie and waved good-bye to the search party.

After a short walk in the woods, Pooh and his friends discovered a clue.

"Look!" cried Roo. "It's Piglet's scarf!"

"Oh, my!" exclaimed Pooh. "You know, Piglet's scarf never goes anywhere without Piglet."

"This is more serious than I thought," said Rabbit.

Meanwhile, the weather had turned windy and cold. Everyone was worried about Piglet. Rabbit turned the pages of the scrapbook to Piglet's drawing of the cold winter day when they tried to build a house for Eeyore.

"Oh, it's a lovely tale," said Rabbit, pointing to the picture.

"Is this story about Piglet, too?" asked Roo.

"Why, yes, Roo, it is," said Pooh. "He seems to be the hero of every story!"

Then Pooh and his friends told Roo the story.

One cold day in the Hundred-Acre Wood, Pooh decided that it was time to build Eeyore a house.
"Where shall we build it?" asked Piglet.
"Well, right here!" Pooh announced. "And since this is where I thought of it, we shall call this place Pooh Corner!"

Soon Tigger joined Pooh and Piglet. He showed them a nearby pile of sticks that was perfect for building a new house. What Pooh, Piglet, and Tigger didn't know was that this pile of sticks was the house Eeyore had built for himself the night before!

Pooh, Tigger, and Piglet brought the sticks to Pooh Corner and started building Eeyore's new house. But several times—just when they thought it was finished—the whole house collapsed.

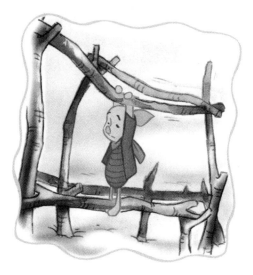

"Oh, bother," said Pooh.

"I suspectorate there's something definitely wrong with these sticks," said Tigger. "All we wanted was for Eeyore to have his own house."

"Eeyore could come and live with me," Pooh said.

"Let's go give ol' Donkey Boy the good news!" said Tigger.

With that, Pooh and Tigger ran off, leaving poor Piglet behind.

Soon after, Pooh and Tigger met Christopher Robin, who had just finished making a Snow-Pooh.

"Look what I made!" said Christopher Robin.

Suddenly the Snow-Pooh shook. Then Eeyore's head popped out.

"Weren't you awfully cold under there?" asked Pooh.

"I've been colder," said Eeyore. "Last night, for instance, it got downright freezing. So I did it. I built myself a house. Just a leaky pile of sticks."

"Did you say sticks?" asked Pooh, a little worried.

Then Piglet came along. Piglet led Eeyore, Pooh, and Christopher Robin to the new house he had built for Eeyore.

"Welcome home, Eeyore," said Piglet as he showed Eeyore the house.

"It's my house all right," said Eeyore. "But I'm sure this isn't where I built it!"

"But I . . . ," began Piglet.

"I suppose the wind must have blown it over here," said Eeyore.

"Hooray for Eeyore's house!" they all shouted. And then Piglet showed them the sign he had made that read Pooh Corner.

"And that's the story," finished Pooh.

"You mean Piglet built Eeyore's house all by himself?" asked Roo.

"That's just how much Piglet cares," said Pooh.

The weather had become stormy. Tigger and Rabbit were getting stormy, too! They both wanted the scrapbook.

"Hand it over, Bunny Boy!" said Tigger. "Finding piglets is what tiggers do best!"

"It's what rabbits do best!" argued Rabbit.

"Tiggers!" yelled Tigger, pulling on the scrapbook.

"Rabbits!" shouted Rabbit, as he tugged back.

Tigger and Rabbit pulled so
hard that Piglet's scrapbook fell
over the bridge!

"Oh, nooooo!" cried Rabbit.

"There goes our map!" said Tigger.

"And Piglet's memories," said Pooh.

Pooh and his friends watched Piglet's drawings
float down the river and wondered how they were
going to find him. They went back to Piglet's house
to get in from
the storm and
decide what to
do next.

Once they were snug in Piglet's house, Pooh and his friends began to draw pictures of their lost friend. Their pictures showed how brave, kind, and delightful Piglet was. Soon the group hung their drawings and hurried out to find their friend.

"PIGLET!" they called out.

"Oh, look what I've found!" shouted Rabbit.
"It's one of Piglet's scrapbook pages," said Pooh.

The wind had blown Piglet's scrapbook pages everywhere. The friends raced around trying to catch them.
"Maybe we can put Piglet's scrappitybook back together," said Tigger.
"Then we can find him in no time!" said Pooh.

Sure enough, they
soon found the scrapbook
itself . . . hanging over a
big waterfall! Bravely, Pooh
climbed out onto a hollow log that stuck out over the
waterfall. *WHOOSH!* Pooh slipped and fell through a
hole in the slippery log. Suddenly he was dangling
over the waterfall where the scrapbook had been—held
only by his shirt.

Quickly, his friends tried to help. They stretched out
over the edge of the cliff holding on to one another
with all their strength. Tigger held out his tail for Pooh
to grab. But it didn't quite reach.

"Pooh!" shouted Tigger. "What are you waiting for?"
"The rescue rope isn't rescuing," Pooh yelled back.
"We just need a little help," suggested Roo.
"Oh, dear," groaned Rabbit. "Who can help?"

To everyone's surprise,
Piglet arrived!
"Hang on, Pooh!"
shouted Piglet as he scooted over his friends.
"Oh, I'm hanging," answered Pooh.
Piglet clutched Tigger's tail, leaned out, and
grabbed Pooh's paw. Then he pulled with all his might.
But just as Piglet pulled Pooh to safety, the log broke.
"*WHOAAHH!*" cried Pooh and Piglet.
The log tumbled down the huge waterfall!

"OH, NO!"
exclaimed Rabbit.
"Uh-oh," said Eeyore.

Rabbit, Roo, Eeyore, and Tigger looked down. They thought that Piglet and Pooh were lost forever!

"We-we never got to tell Piglet how we feel about him," said Rabbit sadly.

"Or Pooh," sniffled Roo.

"Should have told them when we had the chance," sighed Eeyore.

Tigger offered Rabbit his tail to blow his nose on.

"Thank you, Tigger," sobbed Rabbit.

Suddenly Pooh and Piglet rolled out of the end of the hollow log.

"Pooh! Piglet!" cried Tigger. "Oh, we're so glad to see you."

"Glad to see me?" asked Piglet shyly.

"Yeah, we've been following your memories all over the Hundred-Acre Wood," explained Roo. "And they led us right to you."

"Too bad they're all floating down the river," said
Eeyore.

"Ah, the scrapbook's not that important," said Piglet.

"But it showed us the great things you've done,"
said Pooh. "Let's tell him, everyone."

"No, let's show him," Roo suggested.

The friends led Piglet back to his house to show
him their drawings.

"They're wonderful!" said Piglet, looking at the
pictures. "I'm so big!" murmured Piglet.

"Well, of course you are," said Pooh.

"Why, you're a double XL," Tigger declared.

Piglet smiled. He felt big and important.

"I'd say this calls for a celebration!" said Pooh.

"Hoo-hoo-HOO! A Piglet-y party," Tigger cried.

And so
they threw a wonderful
party to celebrate their special friend.

Roo played Pin the Tail on the Donkey.

"Ouch!" cried Tigger, when Roo accidentally
pinned the tail on Tigger.

"Oops, sorry," Roo said.

Everyone laughed—even Eeyore. They were happy
to have their brave, kind, and lovable Piglet back.

Then Pooh took Piglet by the hand and led him to Pooh Corner for a surprise. Pooh had changed the sign so that it read Pooh and Piglet Corner.

"From now on, you shall be a big part of all our plans," Pooh told his happy, little friend.